For Rachel
M. G.

First published in 1993
Text copyright © Margaret Greaves, 1993
Illustrations copyright © Teresa O'Brien, 1993

The right of Margaret Greaves and Teresa
O'Brien to be identified as the Author and the
Illustrator of this work has been asserted by them
in accordance with the Copyright, Designs and
Patents Act 1988.

Typeset by Deltatype Ltd, Ellesmere Port
Printed in Italy
for J. M. Dent & Sons Ltd
Orion House
5 Upper St Martin's Lane
London WC2 9EA

A catalogue for this book is available from the
British Library.

The illustrations for this book were prepared
using pen and ink and water colour.

HENRY IN THE DARK

Margaret Greaves

Illustrated by Teresa O'Brien

Dent Children's Books
London

Henry was very snug in the cat basket with Dizzy and Tizzy and Joseph and their mother. But when the kitchen light was switched off he could see another world outside. There was a bright round moon, and the tree in the garden was full of pale light and moving shadows.

Henry could see something else. Someone had forgotten to close the small top window. He wriggled out of the basket. The others were too sleepy to notice him. He jumped up onto the flat space by the sink and gazed out, his tail twitching with excitement. He crouched, and then with a spring, a scuffle and a slither he was out through the open window.

He had never been out in the dark before.

"How big and strange the world is!" said Henry. "I'm going to explore."

He saw his little black shadow and tried to catch it. But the shadow only danced beside him, so Henry danced with it. The silver moonlight glittered in his eyes.

"I'm going to explore the big world," he said to his shadow. "You come too."

Beyond the garden, light shone from the uncurtained window of another house. Henry trotted over, jumped onto the window-sill, and looked in. Inside the room three excited kittens were chasing a ball all over the floor.

"Miaow, miaow!" squeaked Henry, longing to join in.

Nobody heard him, so he jumped down and prowled round the garden.

He found some potted
plants on a terrace.
  "How kind of someone!"
said Henry. "A whole row
of little pots just the right
size for me to play in."

He put his front paws into one of the smallest pots. Then one hind paw. But when he lifted the fourth paw the pot fell over on top of him.

"Miaow!" squeaked Henry, shaking the soil out of his paws. "How surprising the world is!"

He licked himself clean, then trotted off to explore further.

He found a backyard. In one corner was a rubbish sack with a tear in its side. Some very interesting smells came from the sack. Henry put in a paw and made the hole bigger. He dragged out a piece of paper and chased it over the moonlit yard. The wind caught the paper and made it fight back, which was very exciting.

At last the paper escaped and sailed away, so Henry went back and poked again at the rubbish sack. All sorts of bits came out, including a bone with some meat on it. He sniffed the bone but didn't like it much.

"EeeeYOW!" A long thin alley cat was glaring at him.

"EeeeYOW!" snarled the big cat again. "Little thief, this is *my* yard at nights. And that bone is mine too."

"Please," said Henry, "I don't want it. I'm only exploring."

"You can't explore here. OUT!"

The cat leaped down, and Henry turned and bolted. He ran and ran until he had to stop for breath. His heart was beating dreadfully fast.

"How scary the world is!" said Henry. "I don't want to explore any more. I want to go home. But where *is* home?"

Everything looked strange in the moonlight. Things rustled in the hedge. What was lurking in the patches of black shadow? He was a very small explorer and the world was very big. Suddenly Henry saw his very own apple tree, and with a quick wriggle under the gate he was back in his garden.

"I've got lots to tell the others," he said joyfully, as he scampered to the glass doors of the sitting room. But the doors were shut and the curtains drawn.

"Miaow, miaow!" mewed Henry. "It's me. I'm back. Let me in."

But no one heard him. Perhaps, he thought, they don't even want me any more. At that he opened his mouth till his little pink tongue showed, and wailed at the top of his voice.

Still no one heard him, even though he scrabbled at the glass with his paws.

Then Henry had a good idea.
  He stretched up on his hind legs as far as he possibly could,
and beat both front paws against the glass.
  Bump, bump, bump, bump.

Next moment someone drew back the curtains and opened the doors. Henry scurried inside.

"Why, it's Henry! However did he get out? And what a clever kitten to knock to come in!"

Henry purred loudly. He knew he was clever.

Two minutes later he was drinking a big saucer of warm milk that was very comforting to an explorer glad to be home again.

Then he pushed into the cat basket among the other kittens. His mother was so pleased to see him back that she forgot to be cross.

"Wherever have you been, Henry?" asked Dizzy, waking up suddenly.

"What's it like outside at night?" asked Joseph. He sat up, bright with curiosity.

"Hush! Go to sleep," said their mother. "It's long past your bedtime."

"Did you have an adventure?" asked Tizzy.

"Of course I did. I'm an explorer, and explorers have *lots* of adventures. I'll tell you about them tomorrow. Take your foot out of my ear, Dizzy."

Henry meant to explore a lot more in the morning, but now it was good to be safe and warm with the others. Pushing further in, he turned round twice, put his paws over his nose, and was fast asleep. Explorers get very tired!